Praise for
Connor the Courageous Cutter

"Connor and friends have become part of our bedtime routine and provided many valuable lessons. A positive and refreshing series that will be passed on for years to come!"

—Sam and Amy Curtis

"The books have become nightly bedtime readings for our son. We talk about being there for our friends, especially in times of need, and keeping the faith that good will prevail. Connor's stories resonate with how we feel everyone should treat one another."

—Karen Steffel Kunc

"Connor the Cutter helps teach valuable life lessons to our children. My grandchildren love the book series and we all look forward to the upcoming animated series!"

—Raymond J. McCauley

www.mascotbooks.com

The Adventures of Connor the Courageous Cutter: Mystery of the Baffling Blackout

For more information, please contact:
Mascot Books
620 Herndon Parkway #320
Herndon, VA 20170
info@mascotbooks.com

Library of Congress Control Number: 2018906178

CPSIA Code: PRT0718A
ISBN-13: 978-1-68401-817-8

Printed in the United States

The Adventures Of
CONNOR
THE COURAGEOUS
CUTTER
Mystery of the Baffling Blackout

by Scott McBride
& Rodger Thompson

Illustrated by Brian Martin

T620

Journey with me to a place far away,
Across the seas, and beyond the bays.

Through the big river basins, and just past the capes,
There's a place full of boats of all sizes and shapes.

Come hear their tales, come gather 'round.
And take a voyage with me, to Serendipity Sound!

- Anna the Lighthouse

It was a foggy autumn evening in Serendipity Sound as Felipe the Fishing Trawler dragged his nets for a late-day catch. Connor the Cutter and all of the other boats floated at their piers, anxiously awaiting the arrival of Francis the Freighter.

Simon the Submarine cruised by with a mischievous grin on his face. "Hey, topsiders! Whatcha doing?"

"None of your business," sneered Yardly the Yacht. "Does your kind not understand manners?"

"Yeah," Barry the Barge laughed. "Why don't you go back down below with them other sinkers! We're waiting for Francis the Freighter to bring us some gas before we're all bone dry."

Connor didn't know Simon, but he couldn't help but notice how sad he looked as he slowly sank below the surface.

Just then, Anna's light went out, followed by all of the lights throughout the sound.

Naomi the News Chopper swooped down and announced, "This just in: the power's out on the whole island!"

Barry the Barge spoke up, "Not good. My tank is almost empty and without Anna the Lighthouse, ol' Francis won't be able to find the channel."

"Something or someone must have messed with the power cables beneath the water to cause the blackout," Grayson the Tug-N-Tow speculated.

"By George," Yardly proclaimed. "This sounds like a mystery. If there is one thing I know how to do well, it's solve a mystery."

"If something bad has happened," Connor added, "you may need my help. Count me in!"

Yardly and Connor set out in search of the source of the power outage. As they rounded a bend, they came across Thaddeus the Tugboat, fast asleep, floating out into the sound.

"Look just there, Connor," Yardly said. "Thaddeus's lines have been cut—he's been set adrift! Help me, won't you?"

"I'm on it!" Connor affirmed.

The two of them pushed Thaddeus back to his pier and secured his lines.

"It would take something strong to cut those lines. A large blade or...a claw..." Yardly speculated.

Connor thought hard. "Doesn't Simon the Submarine have a claw hook?"

"Indeed, my dear boy!"

Just then, the loud horn of an incoming freighter echoed in the distance.

Suddenly, Faith the Fireboat rushed up to Connor and Yardly in a tizzy.

"Ewwwwwww! Get it off! Get it off!" she yelled.

On her deck, a large jellyfish was sliming about, trying to find its way back into the water.

"Hold on, Faith," Connor said, giving her a nudge. She listed to the right, and the jellyfish slid into the water with a splash.

"My dear, what nefarious thing happened here?" Yardly asked.

"I was stowing away my hoses when something threw this jellyfish out of the water at me. It's so dark, I couldn't see who it was. That jellyfish almost stung me!"

"Threw, you say?" Yardly echoed. "First the power, then Thaddeus, and now this jellyfish business. By George, I think we have a prankster in our midst!"

A prankster? Connor thought. *These pranks are not nice and someone could get hurt!*

Off in the distance, Francis's horn bellowed. But this time it was louder…closer.

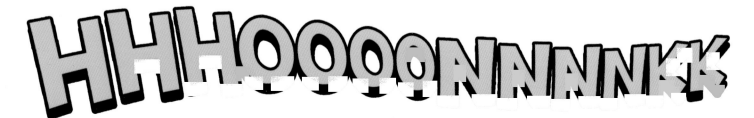

High above the sound, Naomi saw a dark shadow with a few lights lurking just beneath the water, heading out of the channel.

"Good evening, this is News Chopper 6 with a live report!" she broadcasted. "Is Simon the Submarine to blame for the bizarre power outage? Updates at 11!"

Connor heard the announcement and radioed Naomi. "Naomi, it's Connor. Yardly and I will track down Simon and see what he knows. We need you to fly out to Francis and tell him not to enter the port until the power comes back on!"

"Yesssserrrendipity!" Naomi yelled as she flew off toward the horizon.

"I always knew it was Simon," Yardly grumbled. "Submarines are not to be trusted, you see. They don't behave like us boats. Come on, Connor, he's got to be around here somewhere."

"Don't you think you are being a little too hard on Simon?" asked Connor as he searched the area with his spotlight. "I agree that Simon's pranks aren't always funny, but just because he's a little different from us, doesn't mean he's bad, does it?"

Just then, Simon the Submarine popped up in front of Connor. "You must be new around here," Simon said with a frown. "Boats like him have never liked subs like me."

"We know it was you who cut the power!" Yardly declared. "I'm reporting this to the Harbor Master posthaste. You're going to dry dock for eternity if I have my say."

"What? No!" Simon cried. "It wasn't me, I didn't do nothing!"

"Well, someone turned off the power," said Connor. "How do you explain Thaddeus's cut lines or the jellyfish?"

"You're the only one with a claw," Yardly scoffed. "And the only one who can reach the power cables under the water. Explain that, Simon."

"I...I..." Simon stuttered. "I was just trying to be funny, you know, to...to make friends." He looked down toward the water. "But I promise I didn't do anything to the power."

"We'll see about that," said Yardly. "You need to leave right this minute. We don't like your kind around here! Go, before I call the Harbor Master about the mess you've made of things."

Simon quickly submerged and headed out to sea.

As Connor and Yardly headed back to the sound, Connor couldn't help but feel a little confused. He barely even knew Simon, but he did know how tough it was to make friends. He remembered when he first arrived in the sound, and how he was so worried no one would like him. He had to speak up.

"You shouldn't treat others like that, Yardly," Connor said. "Simon's one of the Harbor Master's boats, just like you and me. He was only trying to make friends."

"Hardly like you and me, Connor," Yardly said with a scoff. "And he's not going to make many friends pulling pranks like those."

Just then, Felipe cruised up to the other boats, whistling a merry tune. "Good evening, my friends. A most strange and foggy night for a blackout, yes? I feel as though I have a good catch tonight. The Harbor Master will be pleased, my nets are quite heavy!"

Felipe struggled under the weight of his nets as he pulled them out of the water. "*Ay-ay-ay!* What is that?!"

A large cable spitting electricity and sparks came up from the water, tangled in Felipe's nets.

Barry the Barge jumped back. "Is that some kinda jumbo electric eel?"

Connor shook his bow. "No...it's...it's an electrical cable!"

"Oh no!" Felipe blushed. "I must've snagged an underwater power cable with my nets. How foolish of me. I'm to blame for the blackout. I'm sorry, *mis amigos.*"

Yardly looked at Connor before casting his gaze down into the dark water. "Simon really didn't do it," he said quietly.

Felipe examined the cable. "How do we fix this? Francis needs to pull in before everyone runs out of fuel."

"A cable like this?" Yardly said. "It must be reattached under the water. The only thing that can fix this is—"

"A submarine!" Connor exclaimed. "Come on Yardly, we need to find Simon!"

In the channel, Connor and Yardly spotted William the Sea Plane in the sky and flagged him down to see if he knew which way Simon had gone.

William landed and floated to a stop. "Well, I tell ya—he coulda gone this way or he coulda gone that way, but Gangplank Grotto is what I thought I heard him say."

Yardly looked terrified. "Gangplank Grotto? Count me out! That's far away from Beacon Island, where scoundrels and troublemakers hang out."

"Then we need to stop him before he gets there!" Connor called out. "I'm going with or without you, Yardly!"

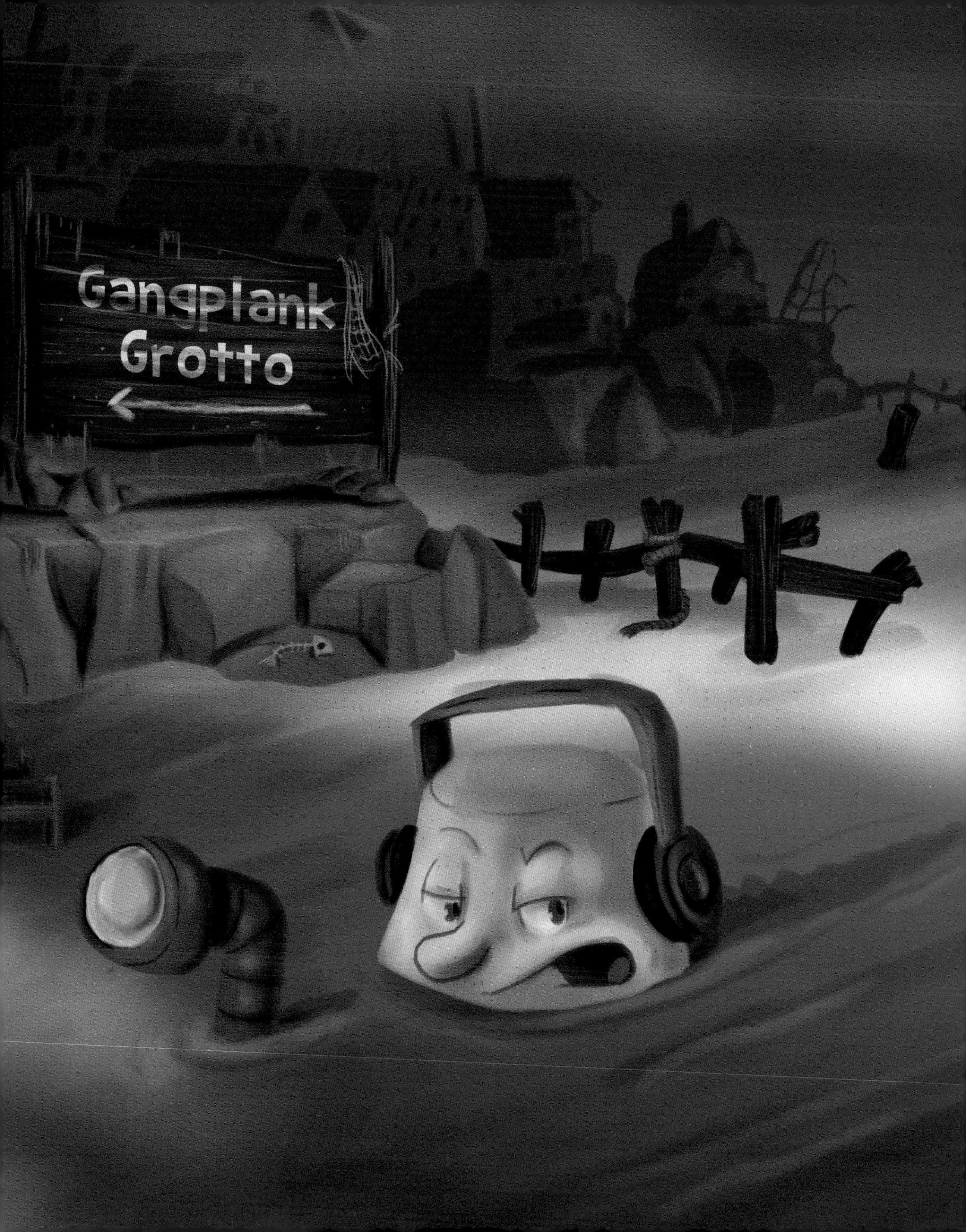
Gangplank
Grotto

Just beyond Beacon Island, Connor saw Simon's periscope
above the surface. "Simon!" he called.

Simon slowly emerged from the water. "Leave me alone."

"We know you didn't turn off the power!" Connor yelled. But
Simon kept going toward Gangplank Grotto. "Simon, we're
sorry! Felipe accidentally cut the power line while dragging
his nets. We're sorry for how we treated you, it wasn't right."

Simon stopped and turned around. "But…I'm not like you guys," Simon said. "You said I'm not welcome in the sound. Why should I stay? No one likes me here."

Connor smiled with a big grin. "You are welcome in Serendipity Sound, Simon. The Harbor Master wants *all* of his vessels to be happy there, not just the ones above the water. We need you right now so Francis can enter the port safely and bring us fuel. The one thing that makes you different is what makes you special. You're the only one who can fix the power. You'll be a hero!"

Simon grew excited. "A hero like you?"

Connor shook his bow. "If I was a real hero, I would have never let the other boats treat you so badly. I'm sorry, Simon."

Simon gave a small smile. "It's okay, Connor. I forgive you... well, what are we waiting for? We've got a cable to fix!"

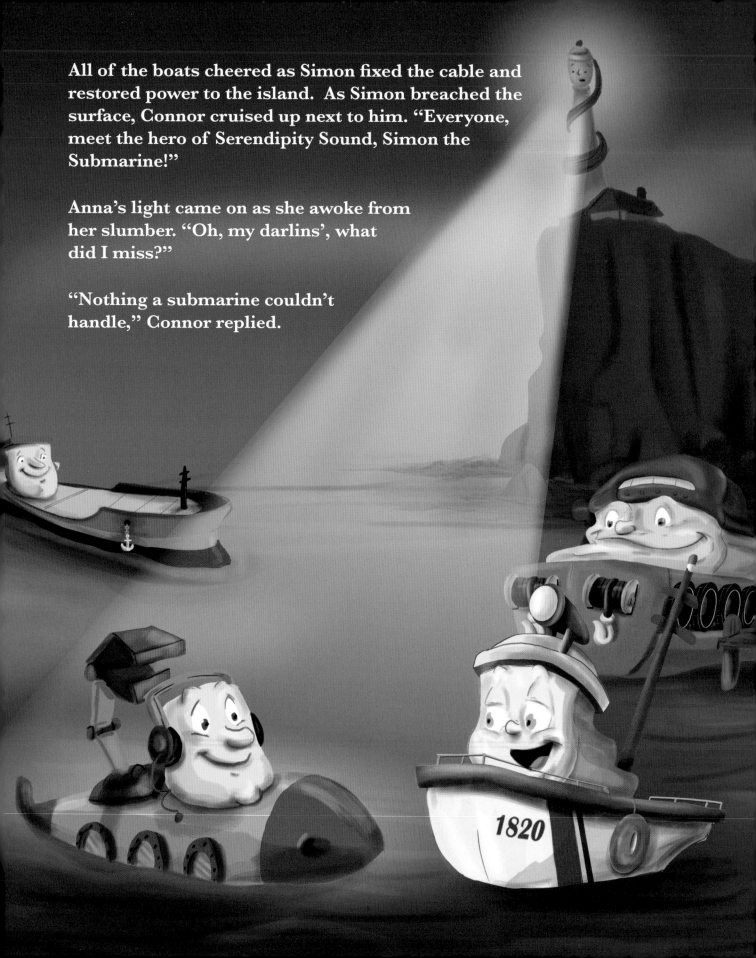

All of the boats cheered as Simon fixed the cable and restored power to the island. As Simon breached the surface, Connor cruised up next to him. "Everyone, meet the hero of Serendipity Sound, Simon the Submarine!"

Anna's light came on as she awoke from her slumber. "Oh, my darlins', what did I miss?"

"Nothing a submarine couldn't handle," Connor replied.

1820

By the beam of Anna's light, Francis the Freighter safely entered the sound, while Connor and all of his pals gave Simon the Submarine a hearty Serendipity Salute.

TOOT TOOT!